Silverlake Fairy School

Unicorn Dreams

Pocket ⇒

Silverlake Fairy School

A magical world
where fairy dreams come true

Silverlake
Fairy School
Unicorn Dreams

LEVEL 3 LINDSAY

Lindsay, Elizabeth.

Unicorn dreams

For Susie V., who loves fairies!

First published in 2009 by Usborne Publishing Ltd., Usborne House,
83-85 Saffron Hill, London EC1N 8RT, England.
www.usborne.com

A CIP catalogue record for this book is available from the British Library.

UK ISBN 9780746076804 First published in America in 2011 AE.
American ISBN 9780794530624 JFM MJJASOND/11 01558/1
Printed in Dongguan, Guangdong, China.

Contents

Chapter One

A Secret

Lila swam beneath the rippling water, supple as a fish, her purple hair flowing over folded wings. Her purple fingernails sparkled as she broke the surface and took a deep breath. It was time to go. The sun was higher in the sky than she expected, and Cook would be upset if she arrived late in the palace kitchen.

On the riverbank, Lila shook a rainbow of water droplets from her wings and squeezed out her hair and threadbare gossamer dress.

Unicorn Dreams

Am I really clever enough to try out for Silverlake Fairy School? she wondered. It was a question on her mind a lot at present. A decision had to be made. It was the best school in fairyland, after all. *Cook thinks I'm good enough, but I'm not so sure,* she said to herself. She stretched her shimmering wings. Soon they would be strong enough to carry her high into the sky. She was about to try a little flutter when she realized somebody was watching her.

A silver-white unicorn stood on the far side of the palace lawn, where a moment ago there had been nothing. On his forehead a golden horn glinted in the early-morning sun. Lila could hardly believe what she was seeing. His mane and tail were the exact same purple as her hair; his hooves the identical sparkling tones of her fingernails. Surely unicorns were silver-white all over? The unicorn returned her gaze with an interested gleam in his eye, until, with a stamp and a snort, he vanished.

Lila sped across the grass, half flying, half running, to the place where the unicorn had been. There were hoof prints, but none came from anywhere or went anywhere. It was amazing! She folded her wings and raced toward the palace, desperate to tell someone about what she had seen. She sped along the gravel walkway, through the stable yard, to the servants' entrance. There she bumped straight into her best friend, Mip, the shoeshine elf.

"Lila, where've you been? Cook's been banging pots and pans like there's no tomorrow. You're late."

"Guess what I've just seen," said Lila, grabbing Mip's arm and pulling him behind the door. "A unicorn!"

"You sure?" asked Mip. "You're not making this up, are you?"

"It had a purple mane and tail the same color as my hair, hoofs the same color as my nails

A Secret

and a horn on his head that glowed like fairy gold."

"Honest?" said Mip. "Do you mean it?"

Lila didn't say anything else but dragged her friend toward the kitchen. She burst through the door, pulling him by the sleeve, expecting to find Cook on her own. What she found instead was Cook, with arms folded, bristling with suppressed fury, glaring at the Lord Chamberlain. Her wizened wings were raised above her shoulders. She couldn't use them to fly, being far too stout, but she could use them to impress and she looked formidable.

Lila and Mip stood at attention, not knowing what to do. The Lord Chamberlain never came to the kitchen. Next to the King and Queen, he was the most important person in the land. To Lila, who had never seen him this close up before, he looked scary in his long black robes, with his unsmiling eyes and thin lips. The Lord Chamberlain fingered the golden chain of state that hung over his chest. His wings too were raised, but neatly folded, his expression cold and aloof.

"Do not get uppity with me! You have been warned," he said to Cook, glancing in Lila's direction. "Think carefully about what I have said."

"I don't need to think. May the best fairies win," said Cook, flinging wide her arms and releasing a spray of exploding flour balls. The Lord Chamberlain quickly retaliated with a shield charm, which sent the flour balls bouncing back across the kitchen table, saving his dark robes from attack.

With a haughty twitch he walked toward the great door leading to the palace staterooms. It swung open to let him through. On his way out he fixed his gaze on Lila for a brief moment, as if trying to work out something he didn't have an answer for. She quickly curtsied. He swept out and the door closed behind him. Better late than never, Mip took off his cap and bowed. Cook scowled.

"Of all the nerve!"

"What's happened?"

With Cook in such a fury, Lila's news about the unicorn went right out of her head. She wondered if she had done something wrong.

Cook gave a deep sigh and opened her arms. "Come here, Lila love," she said and enveloped Lila in the biggest of hugs. "We've got some talking to do. Mip, kettle on. This calls for a nice cup of tea."

Nobody said anything until after the tea was made. Cook was thinking. Lila poured the brew and Cook, stirring her cup with a kitchen knife, a thing she would never normally do, broke the silence at last.

"That Princess Bee Balm has got the Lord High and Mighty Chamberlain wrapped around her little finger, she has," said Cook. "Well, it won't make any difference."

Cook heaved herself to her feet, went into the big walk-in pantry and rummaged about inside. Lila and Mip exchanged looks. When Cook came out again she was carrying a large brown paper package. She blew off the dust and put the package on the table. Then, cutting the string, she unwrapped an old wicker basket.

"I've never shown you this before, Lila," she said. "But I'm showing you now as I think it's time. This is the basket the old dragon sea captain found you in, a-drifting far out to sea on the Ocean of Diamond Waters all those years ago. He brought you to me, a tiny, defenseless baby, and I said as I would take care of you forever and always. I've been as good as my word. I didn't even know you were a fairy until you started growing your wings. I thought you were an elfin baby."

A Secret

Lila and Mip looked at the basket with interest. They both knew that Lila had arrived at the Fairy Palace an orphan. Cook had told the story often. But neither of them had seen the basket or knew that Lila had been found far away at sea.

"And this," said Cook, "this is the golden shawl you was wrapped in. The cloth's faded now but I still keeps the basket and the shawl safe."

Lila reached out and touched the silky fabric. There were glittering golden threads woven into the cloth. "I must have been very tiny."

"You were," said Cook. "A poor starved little thing. But I soon fed you up. I'd always wanted a little one of my own. You were a gift from heaven."

Lila flung her arms around Cook's neck and gave her a big kiss.

"You are the best mother an orphan can have," she said.

Cook gently pushed Lila away.

"Enough soppy nonsense," she said. But Lila knew Cook was pleased, by the quivering smile on her lips. "Now listen, Lord High and Mighty says Princess Bee Balm finds having you in the library during her lessons distracting, even though you've been sitting at the back, quiet as a mouse and Tutor Feverfew hasn't said a word. She says she can't concentrate on her Silverlake Fairy School entrance test with you or anybody else there. From today, during the Princess's lessons, the library is out of bounds to everyone." Cook clasped her hands together and looked rebellious. "But it's not only Princess Bee Balm who needs Tutor Feverfew's cleverness. You do too if you're to take the Silverlake Fairy School entrance test. Why, in the name of wooden spoons, should she mind you sitting quietly at the back?"

"That Princess is horrid as moldy, green cheese. She's worried that Lila will do better than her," said Mip.

A Secret

"Possibly she is and possibly she isn't," said Cook. "All I can say is that the Lord Chamberlain's a horrid snob. He thinks studying's too good for a kitchen fairy. He thinks putting you in for the Silverlake Fairy School entrance test is you getting above your station. Well, we'll show him."

Lila's heart quickened at the thought of no more lessons. She'd never pass the entrance test without them. How could she possibly learn all the things she needed to know? She would have to take a chance and break the Lord Chamberlain's rule.

"What if I hid under a table during the Princess's lessons?" she said.

"Don't even think of it," said Cook. "There would be terrible consequences if you were caught."

"Well then," said Lila. "I could fly up to the library window and listen in from outside."

"Oh, goodness me, no!" said Cook, clasping both hands to her bosom. "A ridiculous idea!

Besides, your wings are not strong enough."

Lila stretched both wings and worked them against the air. Slowly she rose up.

"Wow, Lila," cried Mip. "You can fly!"

Lila touched the ceiling with a finger, then suddenly remembered her important news, and came crashing down onto the table among the teacups.

"I forgot to tell you. I saw a unicorn down by the river. With a purple mane and tail."

"Oh, Lila, it's an omen," said Cook. "Unicorns don't show themselves to just anybody. Unicorns bring luck. I'm sure you're meant to go to Silverlake Fairy School. I didn't spend all these years teaching you to read and write and add up just for you to do kitchen accounts. Oh, no! There's nothing like a good education, where you learn real charms and wand mastery."

"I know, Cook, and I've done my best to learn all I can."

A Secret

"Lilac Blossom, we haven't come this far to fail." When Cook used Lila's full name, it meant she was deadly serious. "You will sit the Silverlake Fairy School entrance test and you will pass. I am not withdrawing you from the test, which is what Lord High and Mighty wants. I'm not even considering it. You'll manage without the lessons. You're clever enough. I'm certain of it."

"Perhaps I am," said Lila, although she wasn't at all sure this was true and she came to a silent decision. *My wings are strong enough to fly to the library window. I'll do it. I'll have my lessons in secret.* She put her arms around Cook, gave her a hug, but said nothing.

Chapter Two

Lessons

At first, Lila was excited by her plan. To listen in to Princess Bee Balm's lessons from outside the royal library was an excellent idea. But it seemed much scarier as the time came closer. That evening, when she told Mip what she was going to do, his eyes grew wide as saucers.

"You must be joking," he gasped. Yet Lila was deadly serious. She tried not to think about what would happen if she was discovered.

"Will you help me?"

Lessons

Mip swallowed nervously and nodded.

"Not a word to Cook," Lila said. "I've missed today's lessons, but I'm not missing tomorrow's."

The next morning, as lesson time approached, Lila and Mip crept along the paved pathway that led into the Fairy Palace gardens and arrived underneath the library window.

"You sure you should be doing this?" Mip asked.

"No, I'm not sure, but I'm going to. You want me to pass the test, don't you?"

"It's a shame the library's not on the ground floor," said Mip, looking up the high wall to the window. "But look! You can hide under the ivy. No one will see you."

"Taking down notes is going to be difficult," said Lila.

"You can remember everything," Mip said. "You're good at that."

"Not that good. I want to do really well in the test."

"Course you do," said Mip, handing Lila the scroll and pencil he'd carried for her. "I'll keep watch. If anybody comes, get under the ivy and keep still."

Lila would not have had the courage for what she was about to do if the thought of failing to get into Silverlake Fairy School hadn't been so terrible. She raised her wings, beating them faster and faster until her feet left the ground. Up she flew. It was the highest she had ever flown and it was hard work, but she didn't stop until she reached the library windowsill. She grabbed hold of a handful of ivy and wiggled her way into the foliage. It was the perfect place for peeking through the window. Lila looked down and gave Mip a shaky thumbs up. He did the same back.

Luckily for Lila, Tutor Feverfew liked fresh air, and all the library windows were open. It would be easy to hear what was said. She peered inside.

Lessons

Princess Bee Balm was sitting at her desk, arranging the folds of an elegant gossamer frock of the palest pink. Lila allowed herself the tiniest of sighs. It was a beautiful dress and put her faded blue one to shame. Taking care not to rustle either leaves or paper, Lila propped her scroll on her knee and licked the end of her pencil.

"Today is Geography review," said Tutor Feverfew, adjusting his spectacles. He was a tall, thin fairy, dressed in a faded green suit. He lifted a great globe onto Princess Bee Balm's desk, causing his old bones to click and creak in protest.

"Must it be Geography today? Couldn't it be Fashion?" asked Princess Bee Balm. "Don't you think this pink is perfect for my coloring, Feverfew?"

The tutor cleared his throat.

"I do, Majesty. But Geography it must be if you are to pass the Silverlake Fairy School entrance test. Attention, if you please." And he tapped the globe with his pointing stick. "Today, we will review our own great Fairy Kingdom. These mountains, Majesty, are called…?"

"Um," said Princess Bee Balm, through a barely concealed yawn. "Is it the…um…"

"Come along, now," said Tutor Feverfew, rapping his stick impatiently on the mysterious mountains.

"It might be…then again it might not be the… um…" The Princess began to rearrange the folds of her frock.

"Try to concentrate, Majesty. This is important." From his sleeve, Tutor Feverfew took out a green handkerchief. Princess Bee Balm pouted.

"It might be the…um…" There was a pause. Tutor Feverfew closed his eyes and patted his brow. "Oh, I don't remember."

But Lila did and burst out with, "They're the Eerie Mountains!"

Then she clapped a hand over her mouth and ducked behind the ivy, horrified at what she had done.

"There," said Tutor Feverfew, neatly folding the handkerchief. "You did know the answer. It takes only a little thought and attention."

Lila's heart pounded. Tutor Feverfew might have mistaken her voice for the Princess's, but what would the Princess do? She peeked back inside.

"And who lives in the Eerie Mountains?" continued Tutor Feverfew, pushing the handkerchief back up his sleeve.

"Boggarts," said the Princess, who, with the blackest of frowns, was craning her neck to see who had given the first answer. Lila ducked out of sight again. *Why did I do that?* she groaned to herself.

"Correct," said Tutor Feverfew. "And what can you tell me of boggarts?"

"They're hairy, horrid goblins, and our enemies."

Lessons

"Quite right. And what is this place to the south of the Eerie Mountains?" Once more, the stick tapped against the globe.

"A lake."

"Yes, but its name, Majesty? What is its name?"

"The Great…um…Silver Lake?"

At Lila's next peek she could see Princess Bee Balm looking over her shoulder, first one way, then the other. In the end the Princess could bear it no longer and got up. Lila hunkered down under the ivy and crossed her fingers.

"Majesty, please," begged the exasperated tutor. "Whatever is the matter?"

"Nothing," said the Princess.

"Time is running out. I beg you, sit down and tell me what this island is called."

At last, and without looking out of the window, the Princess did as she was told and turned her attention once more to the globe. Lila breathed a huge sigh of relief. Patiently, Tutor Feverfew continued with his questions, prompting his pupil with most of the answers. From where she sat underneath the ivy, Lila drew a careful map. First she put in the Eerie Mountains and wrote: *Evil boggarts live here*. Next she drew the Great Silver Lake and the island on the far side. On the island she drew a castle and wrote *Silverlake Fairy School*. If she passed the test that was where she would be going to school.

From the lake she drew the River of Sparkling Waters that flowed all the way down the valley to the town of Silver Spires where she lived. She drew the great Fairy Palace in all the detail she could remember, and streets and houses and the landing jetty at the river where the great river barges were moored. She continued with the river, making it flow into the Ocean of Diamond Waters where, long ago, she had been found adrift in a wicker basket. It made her shiver to think of it and doubly shiver to think what a narrow escape she had just had. If Princess Bee Balm had found her outside the window, she would have been in such trouble.

Lila decided it was time to go before she was discovered. She leaned out from her perch and dropped the pencil. It landed close to Mip. Lila signaled to him to catch the scroll as well, which he did.

In the library, Princess Bee Balm was also drawing a map, and her tutor, leaning over her shoulder, was pointing out mistake after mistake.

"Tutor Feverfew," said the Princess, irritably, "there is somebody in the library. I heard them just now. Search them out."

"No, no, Majesty, only your good self and I," said the tutor, peering shortsightedly between the bookshelves to make sure.

"I heard a voice, I tell you. I will not have anybody eavesdropping on my lessons. Find them and leave me to finish my map by myself."

"Very well, Majesty," said the tutor, setting off to look.

Lila raised her wings and wiggled from behind the ivy. It was a hurried descent and she landed in a crumpled heap.

"Quick," she said as Mip hauled her up. "Run."

The two of them raced around the palace and through the stables to the kitchen door, where they sat on the step to catch their breath.

"What did you learn?" Mip asked.

"Geography," said Lila and showed him her map. "Starting with the Eerie Mountains and boggarts."

"Scary things, boggarts," said Mip. "Glad I never seen one."

"What do you think they look like?" asked Lila.

And underneath the map they took turns to draw one. They gave the boggart big teeth dripping with slime, a hairy body, long hairy arms with claws, narrow eyes and short stumpy legs.

Lessons

They gave him a club to carry. He looked nasty, horrid and just right. Cook came out for a breath of fresh air and found them practicing boggart snarling.

"You don't ever want to meet one of them," she said. "Thank goodness for fairy charms. They keep those evil creatures in the Eerie Mountains. Otherwise they'd be doing their best to steal every ounce of fairy gold in the land."

Lila showed Cook the map and Cook tested her.

"Very good, my girl. If you keep learning at this rate, you'll pass the entrance test easy as winking. See, I told you you didn't need the Princess's lessons. You're doing really well by yourself. In we go, then. There's dishwashing to do and, Mip, you've a pile of boots to clean higher than the topmost Eerie Mountain."

Lila rolled up her scroll and followed the others into the kitchen. She had never had any secrets from Cook before and it felt terrible. But Lila wasn't going to stop listening in on Princess Bee Balm's lessons. She was determined to get into Silverlake Fairy School and nothing was going to get in her way.

Chapter Three

The Angry Cloud

For the next four mornings Lila flew up to the library window and eavesdropped on Princess Bee Balm's important review lessons. She made careful notes on her scroll and kept quiet, even when longing to give an answer. Mip kept a lookout below, and if he saw anyone coming, he would put his fingers between his teeth and blow three chirrups like a sparrow. At the signal, Lila would hide in the ivy and wait for Mip to give the all clear.

Unicorn Dreams

Usually, the visitor was the potting-shed elf, arriving with a wheelbarrow full of manure, or the head gardener, a deaf old gnome, whose greatest love was tending and feeding the Fairy King and Queen's roses in preparation for Royal Rose Day. Shoveling the manure did not take the elf very long, but the old gnome lingered for ages, dusting leaves and talking to his beautiful blooms.

One interruption had meant that Lila had been unable to write down anything on charms to repel boggarts until the gardener had gone. When he had done so, she quickly scribbled the notes, but wasn't at all sure she'd remembered everything correctly. She hoped it wouldn't come up in the test. Still, not being discovered was the most important thing.

On the fifth morning, the day before the Silverlake Fairy School entrance test, rain splashed into the stable yard, making huge puddles. It was the day Tutor Feverfew was going to review how to do the three basic charms every fairy would need to know in order to pass the exam. This was an important lesson that Lila had missed. It was also Royal Rose Day, which was why the Lord Chamberlain had magicked a downpour charm. The gardener's plants always looked their best after a good watering.

"Today's the last day for studying," said Cook, looking out at the gray sky. "Best do it indoors and keep out of the way. When the rain stops, the Royal Rose Day inspection will begin. After that there'll be the banquet. We're going to be busy in the kitchen all day." Cook went over to the shelf for her favorite book of recipe charms – *Feasts for a King*.

"Their Royal Majesties will pass right under the library window," whispered Mip.

"I'll be safe among the ivy," Lila whispered back. "They won't see me. I can't miss today. It's the three basic charms. I must know them for the test."

"Mip, you can help Lila with her studying," said Cook, her nose in the recipe book. "Make yourselves scarce. I've a feast to prepare."

The moment Cook's back was turned Mip grabbed an umbrella and he and Lila hurried from the kitchen. Mip hung the umbrella from his arm with an impish grin.

"You want to watch out," said Lila. "That umbrella has a mind of its own. I've seen Cook have trouble with it. It's a hand-me-down, unpredictable umbrella that one is."

"I'm not afraid of it," said Mip.

"Well, don't say I didn't warn you," said Lila, who always avoided using it.

Opening up the big, black umbrella, Mip stepped outside into the rain. Water pattered and bounced onto the fabric, which turned a holly-leaf green.

"It's behaving," he said.

Lila tucked her scroll under her arm and took

The Angry Cloud

shelter next to Mip. Together they hurried around the Fairy Palace to the garden and the library window. Everything was getting a thorough soaking, including Lila as she stepped out from underneath the umbrella. She stretched her wings and took off. Her days of practice had made her much better at vertical flying and she reached the windowsill in no time.

The library windows had been pulled almost shut to keep out the wet, and the splattering rain made it difficult to hear what Tutor Feverfew was saying. Lila looked inside in time to see three words arrange themselves on the lesson board. *Three Basic Charms.* Lila struggled with her scroll and tried to write down the heading, but the paper was wet and her pencil wouldn't work. She huddled under the ivy and peered in at the board.

"May I remind you, you will have to demonstrate one of the following three charms in the practical wand test. The first is *levitation*," said Tutor

Feverfew, tapping the board with his pointing stick. The word "levitation" appeared. "Firstly, Majesty, what does this word mean?"

Princess Bee Balm puckered her lips and made a pretense of thinking. Lila was certain that it was something to do with things floating in the air.

Tutor Feverfew sighed and made several up-and-down movements with his pointing stick. He let go and the pointing stick floated where he had left it.

"A clue," he offered.

"Oh," said Princess Bee Balm. "It means things rising into the air."

"Well remembered, Majesty," said Tutor Feverfew taking back the stick. "Progress! And how do the wand movements for making things rise into the air go?" The Princess made a vague movement with her hand. "No, no, like this. Pay attention, Majesty. *Down, across, up, down.*"

Lila only saw the final stroke. She wished Tutor

The Angry Cloud

Feverfew would move around a bit. But she did see the Princess's scroll rise into the air, guided by the pointing stick, before it dropped back onto the desk. The pointing stick was a wand. Why hadn't she realized this before? She supposed because it was rather plain and this was the first time she had seen Tutor Feverfew do wand magic. When she got her own wand, Lila wanted it to be colorful and glittery with a star or moon or magical hare on the end. She didn't want a plain white stick like Tutor Feverfew's or a wooden spoon shape like Cook's. Even the Lord Chamberlain's wand, although not glittery, was shaped like a silver snake.

"A demonstration please, Majesty," said the tutor. "Make your scroll float up from the desk."

Princess Bee Balm took the wand.

"*Down, across, up, down,*" she chanted, pointing the wand at her scroll. She tried several times, until at last the scroll fluttered and rose a little.

The Angry Cloud

"Excellent, Majesty. Better than last time. That will be good enough for the wand test. Now, the second practical charm is to make a small breeze." Tutor Feverfew took a large book from one of the shelves and the words "small breeze" appeared on the lesson board. He placed the book on Princess Bee Balm's desk and opened it. "A reminder, Majesty. It's *down, around, around again and point*." A breezy gust came from the end of the wand and turned several pages of the book. Tutor Feverfew shook the wand and the wind stopped. "Your turn, Majesty."

Lila's fingers itched to try it herself and she longed for a real wand of her own. But she would only get one if she was admitted to Silverlake Fairy School. If she didn't get in she would have to wait until she was much older before she would be allowed one. It was one of the great attractions of going to the school. You were presented with your own wand on the first day.

Unicorn Dreams

Princess Bee Balm had no difficulty in making a breeze. *"Down, around, around again and point,"* Lila repeated quietly to herself. There was a break in the clouds at last and the rain had almost stopped. Lila tried to write down the instructions on her soggy scroll, but the paper tore.

"Finally, we have cloud formation," said Tutor Feverfew. "Cloud formation" appeared on the board. "We've had a good demonstration of that today since the gardeners requested rain. Although I think the sun is coming out at last. Let's see if you can make a little cloud in the library, Majesty. I'll remind you of the movements."

Lila watched carefully. *Down, around, down, up and forward thrust.* She could remember that. From the end of Tutor Feverfew's wand grew a fluffy white cloud. It floated across the library toward the window.

"I will release it," he said. By the time the cloud

bumped against the windowpane, Lila was hidden underneath the dripping ivy. The window was pushed wide open and the little cloud floated outside.

Princess Bee Balm joined Tutor Feverfew and together they watched it drift skyward. Lila hardly dared breathe. They only had to turn in her direction and she would be in terrible trouble. She longed to make herself invisible, but that was the kind of advanced magic you only learned at Silverlake Fairy School.

"Now, Majesty, it's your turn," said Tutor Feverfew.

"It's a bit like making a balloon," said the Princess.

"Not at all," tutted Tutor Feverfew. "A cloud is not a bit like a balloon. A cloud will reach the other clouds and merge in with them. A balloon goes pop."

The two of them moved back into the library

and Princess Bee Balm took up the wand.

"*Down, around, down, up, down and forward thrust!*"

"Oh dear me, no!" cried Tutor Feverfew. "One too many downs." But before he could reach the Princess to cancel the charm, he tripped on a chair. "Drop the wand," he cried, tumbling over.

Lila, startled by the crash, leaned out from her hiding place and was hit by the full force of an angry gray cloud. It swirled out of the library window, knocking her from the windowsill and carrying her up with it into the sky.

"Help," she cried. But she quickly disappeared deep inside the cloud and no one could hear her. She beat her wings and struggled through the clinging mist, unable to find her way out. She felt like she was going around and around in circles. At last she broke free into sunshine. It was such a relief. But the feeling didn't last long. Lila looked down and almost fainted with shock.

The Angry Cloud

Far below, two pale faces were looking up from the library window, an inside-out umbrella was dragging an unwilling elf across the grass, and the Royal Rose Day inspection party was strolling toward the rose bed, led by the King and Queen in glinting golden crowns. Lila saw all this in the half second before she started to fall.

Chapter Four

A Secret No More

The wind whistled in Lila's ears and grew louder the faster she fell. She tried to fly but her wings were wet and heavy. She was also upside down. All she could do was wail as she plummeted to earth. A horrible crash seemed inevitable, until she saw, from the corner of her eye, a glint of gold and a streak of purple. Her hands discovered thick strands of mane and to her surprise, she found herself astride a sturdy silver-white back, no longer falling, but riding.

A Secret No More

Lila beat her wings, sending out a spray of sparkling water droplets that arced into a sunlit rainbow. And as they lifted her from the broad silver-white back she let the mane slip from her fingers. Down she came, flying her hardest to slow her fall. Nevertheless, the rose bed came up fast to meet her and she landed on top of a prickly briar, the breath knocked from her body. Above her, voices clucked and tutted.

"Who is she?"

"Did you see the unicorn?"

"It saved her."

"Has she broken a wing?"

"What was she doing in that cloud?"

Lila looked up into the face of the Fairy Queen.

"My dear, are you hurt?"

Struggling to her feet, Lila tried to straighten the rose bush. There was a large rip in her gossamer dress where a trembling knee poked out. She gave up on the bent rose and curtsied as deeply as she could manage without falling over.

"Lilac Blossom, at your service, Your Majesty," she said, her cheeks blushing a deep purple. She had never been this close to Their Royal Majesties before. A sea of noble fairy faces peered down at her.

"I know who she is!" At the sound of the voice, every face turned up to the library window. "It's that kitchen fairy. It was her voice I heard the other day. Little know-all. She's been listening in on my lessons." Princess Bee Balm scowled down at Lila.

"Come, my dear," said the Fairy King to his Queen. "The child is unharmed. We can deal with her later."

"Indeed, Your Majesty, she needs dealing with," said the Lord Chamberlain, looking down his nose at Lila. His words made Lila tremble even more.

A Secret No More

"You're the fairy I've seen swimming in the river. And you have your own unicorn? Most unusual, my dear," said the Fairy Queen. "You are lucky indeed. I should like to know more about him. He matches your distinctive coloring. No doubt we will meet again later."

The head gardener glared at Lila and at his ruined rose bush while the Fairy Queen moved away to continue her inspection. "Oh," she said. "The scent of those red blooms. I can smell them from here."

The head gardener forgot about Lila and gave the Queen a beaming smile. Mip dragged Lila away from the royal party.

"That was lucky," he said. "I saw you go up in the cloud. I didn't think you were ever coming down again."

"I'm in terrible, terrible trouble," groaned Lila. "I could be banished for what I just did."

"No, no," said Mip. "Not for that. Never."

But by his expression Lila could tell he was as worried as she was.

"Better tell Cook," she said and a feeling of dread gripped her tummy.

Back in the kitchen, Cook was in the middle of frantic preparations for the Royal Rose Day feast. Kitchen charms were flying everywhere and fairies from all over the palace were laying out silver platters ready for the delicious treats Cook was creating. Sweet and spicy aromas filled the air, and a group of foot-elves lined up ready to carry the first dishes to the Great Hall. In the middle of the kitchen table was the Royal Rose Day cake, a splendid creation and one of Cook's best. It was three tiers high and covered with delicate iced rosebuds.

Lila and Mip exchanged hopeless glances. Now was not the time to interrupt. Cook was far too

busy. The Royal Rose Day feast was about to begin. The best thing to do was help.

Ages later, Lila and Mip had washed and dried hundreds of plates, knives, forks, spoons and glasses – hard work even with Cook's kitchen charms. By the time the foot-elves came for the cake, their backs were aching and they were swaying with tiredness. Four of the burliest elves carried the great confection through the kitchen door, which closed at last. Wearily Cook said, "Charms at ease. Kettle on. It's time for a nice cup of tea."

All the kitchen fairies were glad to stop, except Lila. Now she must tell Cook what had happened and Cook was not going to be pleased. Slowly Lila crossed the kitchen.

"What is it?" Cook asked, as Lila tugged at her sleeve.

A Secret No More

"I've been discovered listening in on Princess Bee Balm's lessons."

Cook gasped and swayed with shock. Mip pushed a chair into place behind her and she sat down heavily.

"But...but, Lila, you haven't been to the Princess's lessons since the Lord Chamberlain's visit. Have you?" she asked.

"I've been listening in from the windowsill," confessed Lila. "I had to. There are so many books in the library I didn't know which to read on my own. And I didn't want to miss anything. Only, today, Princess Bee Balm made an angry cloud by mistake and it carried me off. My scroll is lost. But the worst thing is that the Princess told everyone what I'd been doing. The Queen said something about meeting me later. Will I be banished?" Lila bit her bottom lip, and Cook slumped across the table.

"This is a pretty pickle," she said, rubbing flour

onto her nose. "Well, you must tell the truth," she declared. "What more can a fairy do? We'll have to wait and see what the King and Queen say. But first, we must make you presentable. If you get summoned, you can't appear before Their Royal Majesties with a rip in your frock."

Mip fetched Cook's sewing basket. By the time she had finished her stitching, the remains of the Royal Rose Day cake had come back to the kitchen. One of the foot-elves gave everyone a piece but Lila was too anxious to eat any. She crossed and uncrossed her legs and chewed her bottom lip. It was horrid worrying about what was going to happen.

"The unicorn," said Mip, nudging Lila. "When you said you'd seen one I didn't believe you. But, wow, it was amazing."

"I wonder where it comes from," said Lila.

"Maybe it can get you out of this tricky spot, too," said Mip.

A Secret No More

"But how?" asked Lila.

Mip couldn't answer that. He sat next to his friend, pushing cake around a plate. He didn't feel like eating anything either.

A sudden hush came over everyone. Stately footsteps could be heard coming closer and closer down the corridor. The door opened and the tall, dark figure of the Lord Chamberlain strode into the kitchen.

"Fairy Lilac Blossom," he boomed. "The King and Queen wish to see you at once. Follow me."

Lila stood up and so did Cook. She took Lila's hand and together they walked toward the door. Lila wondered what punishment was in store.

"Not you, Cook," said the Lord Chamberlain. "Their Royal Majesties have not asked for you." He raised a disdainful eyebrow, and turning swiftly on his heels, returned the way he had come.

Lila followed on alone. Even if the King and Queen didn't banish her from the Kingdom, they were certain to stop her from doing the Silverlake Fairy School entrance test. Nevertheless, she took a deep breath and lifted her head high, even though her hard work had been for nothing and all her hopes were dashed.

Chapter Five

The Test

Lila knew the way along the checkered corridor of statues. She and Mip had often come as far as the entrance to the Great Hall, but they had no idea how to operate the charms to get inside. The Lord Chamberlain had no difficulty. At his approach the huge doors swung wide. All traces of the Royal Rose Day feast were gone and Lila followed him across a vast empty floor to the high thrones at the far end.

The King and Queen were both seated and

beside them was Princess Bee Balm on her own little throne. To the side stood Tutor Feverfew, darting little shortsighted glances hither and thither. Lila noticed with a jolt that the King was holding her scroll. The Lord Chamberlain came to a sudden stop and Lila only just saved herself from cannoning into his back.

"Fairy Lilac Blossom," the Lord Chamberlain announced and bowed. He stepped aside and Lila curtsied. There was a silence while the King regarded her. Lila's heart raced and she stared at the floor.

"Tell us, Lilac Blossom, what were you doing in that cloud?" asked the King.

"Explain from the beginning," added the Queen. "Take your time."

Lila wasn't sure where the beginning was, but she knew the most important part of her story.

"Please, Your Majesties, I'm studying for the Silverlake Fairy School entrance test. I used to sit in on Tutor Feverfew's lessons. I was quiet as a mouse at the back of the library." This revelation caused Tutor Feverfew to give Lila a surprised glance. She carried on. "But since the Lord Chamberlain's new rule about no one being allowed in the library when the Princess is studying, I've been listening secretly from the windowsill. And Tutor Feverfew was teaching the three basic charms and the Princess's cloud swept me away. I'm very, very sorry I ruined the rose bush."

"Listening in on the windowsill, so I hear, so I hear!" said the King. "And does this belong to you?" The King held up Lila's scroll for everyone to see.

"Yes, Your Majesty."

"And has our royal tutor read it?"

"I just have, Your Majesty," said Tutor Feverfew. "The notes are very thorough. This is the scroll of a promising student. I wish that all my students were as hard-working and thorough as Lilac

Blossom." He turned and looked pointedly at the Princess.

A promising student! He meant her, thought Lila. She was pleased until she realized that the Princess was glaring at her with an angry expression. At once she wished Tutor Feverfew had said nothing.

"Yes, Bee Balm," nodded the King. "Your mother and I both feel a little more application to your studies would be a good idea."

"Yes, Papa." The Princess's tone was calm, but Lila could see her pride was wounded.

"Why would you like to go to Silverlake Fairy School?" asked the Queen, looking at Lila.

Lila took a deep breath and ignored the Princess's stare.

"I'd like my own wand and to be able to help protect the Fairy Kingdom from boggarts, and to learn sun and moon and star charms," Lila told her in a rush. "It's Cook's dearest wish that I go and now that I understand some of the things I could learn, it's mine too. If I pass the test my wish will come true."

Princess Bee Balm raised her eyes toward the ceiling and shook her head as if she couldn't believe her ears. Lila blushed. Yet surely the Princess wanted to do these things herself?

"A purple fairy is a rarity, and one that conjures up her own purple unicorn even more so," said the Fairy Queen. "We saw him break your fall, Lilac Blossom. I was impressed."

At the mention of the unicorn, Princess Bee Balm frowned even more. She caught the Lord Chamberlain's eye, then turned to look out of the window.

"Lord Chamberlain, you did not tell us there were any other fairies in the palace taking the Silverlake Fairy School entrance test," the Queen continued.

"Hum!" The Lord Chamberlain cleared his

throat. "I have only recently received the entrance test list, Your Majesty. My apologies." He bowed, his eyes glancing in the Princess's direction. Princess Bee Balm tilted her chin and for a brief moment held his gaze before looking down at her hands folded in her lap.

"Well, my dear," said the King to the Queen. "What should we do?"

"She must take the entrance test along with the other fairies," said the Queen without hesitation.

"So be it," said the King. "That is the royal command. But no more listening in on windowsills, Lilac Blossom. I'm sure Princess Bee Balm would gladly have shared her lessons with you if you had asked."

Lila didn't dare look at the Princess, knowing she would have done no such thing.

The Fairy Queen smiled. "Do you think you could summon your unicorn now, my dear? It would be interesting to see him again."

Her unicorn? Was the magnificent creature really hers? How could that be so? Lila didn't dare ask.

"I'm sorry, Your Majesty, I don't know how," was all she said.

"Of course she doesn't, Mother," said Princess Bee Balm with a glittering smile. "She's only a kitchen fairy."

Lila lowered her head and blushed again.

"Well, if she gets to Silverlake Fairy School, I'm sure she'll learn soon enough," said the Fairy Queen. "Good luck, my dear."

"Don't forget this," said the King, holding out Lila's scroll. "Take it, fairy, and well done."

Lila grabbed her scroll, curtsied and ran out of the Great Hall as fast as she could, glad to be gone from the presence of royalty, especially that of Princess Bee Balm. Lila had never had an enemy before, but it was clear that Princess Bee Balm thoroughly disliked her. What had she done? She couldn't think of a single thing apart from being a

The Test

lowly kitchen fairy and there was nothing she could do about that!

Back in the kitchen, Lila was greeted by a sea of anxious faces. All the servants in the castle appeared to be waiting for her. What a relief it was to feel safe with friends. Her face lit up with a wide smile.

"I can sit the test," she announced and held up her scroll triumphantly. There was a cheer and the elves tossed their caps. Mip's went all the way to the ceiling. Cook crushed Lila in a big bear hug and everyone applauded.

"Wonderful, wonderful news," said Cook, dancing Lila around the table.

"And I've saved you some cake," said Mip grinning from ear to ear, holding out a huge slice.

Lila laughed and took a big bite.

* * *

The test was to be held the next morning in the royal ballroom and fairies were coming from all over the Kingdom to take it. Lila was up early, nervous and excited at the same time. Cook made her eat a bowl of special fairy porridge, although she didn't feel a bit hungry.

"Brain food," said Cook. "It'll give you energy."

After she had finished, Cook and the other fairies and elves gathered around, and Mip handed Lila a little package.

"What is it?"

"Open it and see!"

Lila unwrapped a beautiful rainbow pencil.

"It's for good luck," said Mip. "Tap a color twice and that's the color it will write."

"Thank you," smiled Lila. "What a wonderful present!" She held the pencil tight, certain it would bring her luck.

Once Cook had given her one last hug, Lila went to join the other fairies waiting outside the ballroom. She stood patiently in line until it was her turn to be registered.

"Name," said the fairy at the desk.

"Lilac Blossom."

The fairy looked up at Lila's purple hair and fingernails, and the purple tint of her skin.

"Goodness, we don't often see a fairy like you." She smiled and handed Lila a name tag that perfectly matched the color of her hair. "Stick it to your frock," she said. "Go on in and find a desk. Good luck."

Inside the ballroom, light from the chandeliers reflected in the tall gilt mirrors and made the room appear even bigger than it was. Hundreds of desks were set out, each with a quill, an inkwell and a chair. It was difficult to see where the room ended and where the desks reflected in the mirrors began. Lila walked down the rows looking for a free place. It wasn't until she was nearly at the front that she found one.

Unicorn Dreams

Lila sat down and laid her rainbow pencil beside the quill. The desk next to her had a large card on it which said: *Reserved*. The Lord Chamberlain swished briskly between the rows and removed the notice. Lila's heart skipped a beat when Princess Bee Balm took the place, smoothing creases from her silky frock. Lila fiddled with the sleeve of her old blue dress and smiled shyly at the Princess. But the Princess looked straight through her as if she wasn't there.

There was a sudden flurry of sparkling wings at the front of the ballroom and a glittering orange fairy appeared, carrying a great bundle. She folded her wings neatly and silence fell.

"Good morning, everyone. My name is Mistress Pipit – please remember it's 'Pip' followed by an 'it' to make Pipit. And I am the First Year teacher at Silverlake Fairy School. It's my pleasure to welcome you all here today. The examination you are about to take is in two parts: the first part

The Test

is the written part, the second is the practical wand test. So now I am going to give you your Silverlake Fairy School writing scrolls and question parchments. You will have one hour to complete Part One. Do not begin until I say so. Try not to be nervous, take your time and, fairies, do your best."

With a reassuring smile, Mistress Pipit opened her arms, and scrolls and parchments took off like a flock of white birds. One of each landed neatly on every desk. At the top of Lila's scroll was her name written in elegant purple lettering, which looked so beautiful and important that Lila was proud to be the only purple fairy in the whole room. It was much better than feeling like the odd one out.

"Is there anyone without a question parchment or a writing scroll?" Mistress Pipit asked. After a pause, she continued, "Very well, if you are all ready, your time begins now."

Unicorn Dreams

Lila felt a moment of panic. This test would decide her whole future. What if she didn't know any of the answers? With trembling fingers she turned over the parchment and looked at the questions.

Chapter Six

The Dream Wish

Lila took a deep breath and began to read. Yes, she could describe the three basic charms; yes, she could draw a map of the Fairy Kingdom, marking in the mountains and valleys; yes, she did know that Queen Saffron had been the first fairy in history to perfect an invisibility charm. What a relief! She also knew that a boggart's main aim in life was to steal fairy gold. It was all right, she could do this.

Too shy to ask if she could use her rainbow

pencil, she picked up her quill, dipped it in the inkwell and began to write her answers. Dip, write, dip, write. Blots flew across the scroll but, more importantly, the words flowed. She wrote and wrote.

Then, for some reason, the hairs on the back of Lila's neck prickled. She looked up. At the next desk, Princess Bee Balm had stopped writing and was gazing at something in one of the mirrors. Her lips, half hidden behind her hand, were moving silently. Lila looked down at her scroll. Her carefully written words were rearranging themselves on the page. Then the mixed-up letters faded, leaving no writing at all.

She nearly cried out, but was stopped by the look of triumph on Princess Bee Balm's face. The Princess lowered her head and continued writing. Had the Princess activated a vanishing charm and made Lila's work disappear? How could she possibly know such a thing? Unless...and the look that had passed between the Lord Chamberlain and the Princess in the Great Hall came to mind.

Lila didn't know what to do. Her thoughts raced as she looked at her blank scroll. Would there be time to write out the answers again? But what if the Princess kept making them disappear? Lila had to try; she couldn't hand in a blank scroll. Perhaps, if she swapped the quill for the rainbow pencil, the Princess might not know how to magic away pencil writing. All shyness gone now, Lila put up her hand.

"Please," she whispered to Mistress Pipit when the teacher came over. "Would it be all right if I used my colored pencil? My quill's making a lot of blots."

"I must check it for cheating charms," said Mistress Pipit and held the pencil for a moment. "Yes, that's fine, dear," she said.

Gratefully, Lila took back the pencil and tapped the violet stripe. The Princess, busy writing, didn't look up. Starting again from the beginning, Lila redoubled her efforts. Time was short now. Would the Princess be able to try the charm a second time? The pencil wrote beautifully, gliding across the scroll. Lila worked furiously, hurrying to write her answers all over again while the time ticked steadily by.

"You have ten minutes left," announced Mistress Pipit.

Princess Bee Balm glanced toward Lila, but before she could even think of trying another vanishing charm, Lila's hand shot up.

"I've finished," she said, even though she hadn't, and could have written lots more. She got up and thrust her writing scroll at Mistress Pipit.

"Are you sure?" the teacher asked.

"Yes," said Lila. "The pencil's worked well, don't you think? I hope you like violet writing."

She was desperate for Mistress Pipit to see that her scroll was covered in complete sentences. If the words vanished now, the teacher would know a charm had been used and might be able to undo it. Mistress Pipit looked down at the answers and nodded.

"Sit quietly until the end of the test," she said, running her eye down the scroll before putting it on the examiner's table. Princess Bee Balm didn't look up again, but dipped her quill in her inkwell and carried on writing. Lila sat with her head in her hands, wondering if she had done enough to pass.

"Quills down," said Mistress Pipit, at last. She waved an elegant orange wand, and the scrolls, including Lila's, rolled up and disappeared with a little pop. "After a short break we will continue with the practical wand test. You'll be asked to do this with a partner. A list of the pairings is pinned up outside the ballroom."

After the disaster of the written test, Lila began to panic about using a wand for the first time.

What if she couldn't make it work? She waited until Princess Bee Balm and the other fairies had gone outside before she went to look at the list herself.

The Princess, who must have been the first to find out who she was paired with for the practical test, was arguing with the Lord Chamberlain. He was shaking his head and shrugging his shoulders. *What was she upset about now?* Lila wondered. She stood on tiptoes, peering over the wings and shoulders of the fairies in front of her to see who her partner was. She squeezed closer for a better look.

"I wonder who Lilac Blossom is?" the fairy beside her whispered.

"That's me," said Lila.

"Really? You are lucky! You're with the Princess," said the fairy.

Lila searched for her name and there it was beside Princess Bee Balm's. Her tummy did a somersault. Things were getting worse by the minute. Perhaps Mistress Pipit thought that because she lived at the palace she was a friend of the Princess's. What a joke! But there was nothing to be done.

Lila waited outside in the sunshine with the other fairies. She was getting more and more anxious by the minute. The Lord Chamberlain had gone and the Princess was standing on her own, looking disgruntled.

The first names called were those of Princess Bee Balm and Lila. Watched by everyone, the two fairies had no choice but to walk into the ballroom side by side. Ignoring each other, they curtsied politely while Mistress Pipit marked them off her list. Beside the teacher was a row of colored wands laid out on a long table. Lila was apprehensive, but the thought of trying magic for the first time also filled her with excitement.

"I'd like you each to select a wand," Mistress

Pipit said with an encouraging smile. "Try not to be nervous. I'm not going to ask you to do anything difficult."

Princess Bee Balm chose a wand of the deepest pink that blended perfectly with her wing tips. Lila longed for a purple wand, but the nearest to it was a spindly mauve one with a tiny star at its tip. Mistress Pipit nodded reassuringly and Lila took the slender wand.

"Now, decide which one of the three basic charms you would like to show me. Which one would you like to do, Lilac Blossom?"

"Levitation, please," said Lila.

Mistress Pipit raised an inquiring eyebrow at Princess Bee Balm.

"*I* wanted levitation," said the Princess, pouting.

"There's no rule that says you can't both do the same." Mistress Pipit smiled.

"No, no, I'll do cloud formation," said Princess Bee Balm.

"Very well. Lilac Blossom, choose something in the room you would like to levitate."

"A log," said Lila, her eyes alighting on a huge pile of wood that sat by the great fireplace ready for burning.

"Excellent." Mistress Pipit tapped twice with her wand, making a downward movement toward the floor. At once a log rolled from the top of the pile and floated across the room toward them, coming to rest at Mistress Pipit's feet. "Very well, Lilac Blossom, levitation if you please."

Lila cast her mind back to Tutor Feverfew's lesson, and raised the wand. *Down, across, up, down.* But the wand was dead in her hand. *Down, across, up, down.* Nothing happened. Behind Mistress Pipit's back Princess Bee Balm smiled. Lila felt terrible.

"Have you used a wand before, Lilac Blossom?" asked the teacher.

"No, never, sorry."

"Oh," said the orange fairy. "Then I think you'd better try this before you try the log." An orange feather fluttered down from the ceiling and landed gently at Lila's feet. "You know the moves for levitation. Just let your wrist relax a little more. Yes, that's it. And remember to keep the wand pointing directly at the feather."

Lila recited *down, across, up, down* in her head and pointed the wand carefully. The feather wobbled slowly into the air.

"Well done," said Mistress Pipit, and the feather vanished. "Now try the log."

Down, across, up, down, repeated Lila, buoyed by her success. The log rocked and rose jerkily.

"Wow," said Lila, startled by its ungainly flight. At once the log crashed to the floor and pieces of bark scattered everywhere. "Oh, no," she gasped. "What a mess!"

"Don't worry," said Mistress Pipit and magicked the pieces away.

Unicorn Dreams

"Now, Bee Balm, cloud formation, if you please, dear."

The Princess executed a perfect fluffy white cloud. It grew from the end of the pink wand and floated up to the ceiling, where it bounced happily until Mistress Pipit dissolved it. Princess Bee Balm smiled in her superior way. The Princess might not have been paying attention in her lessons, but she had certainly made up for it with some last-minute cramming. Lila felt cast down.

"And now I would like you both to try a dream wish. Who can tell me what that is?"

Lila had never heard of a dream wish, but Princess Bee Balm had.

"It's making a dream come to life. I did the theory in class."

"Good. Making a dream wish come true is something that can't be taught. You can either do it or you can't. Who would like to try first?"

"Me," said Princess Bee Balm. "I'm sure I can

do it. All you've got to do is think clearly of something, point your wand and it'll appear."

"Then off you go, my dear," said Mistress Pipit.

The Princess pointed the pink wand and closed her eyes. After a few moments of concentration, she opened them again. She looked surprised that nothing had happened.

"What are you wishing for?" asked Mistress Pipit.

"A ballgown," said the Princess. "I thought it would work if I dreamed of something I wanted."

"Why not try something a little simpler?"

"I don't want anything else. I want a ballgown. I know exactly what it should be like. A dark pink color. Why won't my dream wish work? It should. I'm a Princess. It's not fair!" Princess Bee Balm tossed the pink wand back on the table and grumpily folded her arms.

Mistress Pipit turned to Lila and Lila closed

her eyes. She knew what her perfect dream wish would be, but the wand was leaden in her hand. Try as she might, she couldn't do it either.

"Just a moment, wands work at their best when they're the same color as the fairy using them," said Mistress Pipit, and she tapped Lila's wand with her own. At once, the mauve color deepened to a rich purple. The princess sniffed disdainfully but said nothing. Her wand had been an exact color match. "Try now."

Lila's hand tingled and, in her mind's eye, she conjured up the silver-white unicorn, with his purple mane and tail, galloping across the sky. She held up the wand and a mysterious power flowed out of the star at its tip. At that moment the unicorn became more than a dream. Lila opened her eyes, to see him trot across the ballroom toward her. He tossed his head and snorted, and she held him there, pointing the wand until her hand trembled and she could no longer hold out her arm. There was a painful tug at her heart and the unicorn faded away.

"A beautiful dream wish, Lila," said Mistress Pipit, taking the wand and turning it mauve again. "Well done."

Lila, still in awe of what she had done, took a while to notice that Princess Bee Balm kept glancing in her direction, her previous haughtiness gone. Something else had taken its place, although Lila couldn't work out what it was.

"Thank you both very much," said Mistress Pipit. "A letter telling you your results will arrive for each of you tomorrow."

The Princess bobbed a brisk curtsy and hastened out of the ballroom. Lila curtsied too, then followed her out. The dream wish had left her feeling tired and dazed. It had been wonderful to be able to do it, a real achievement, but the mess she had made of the levitation would count against her. And when she thought about the unfinished question paper she shook her head and sighed, sure she had failed the Silverlake Fairy School entrance test.

Chapter Seven

Letters

Back in the palace kitchen everyone wanted to know how she had done.

"Lila, you can't have done that badly," said Cook. But even she was shocked when she heard how much work was lost to the vanishing charm.

"And the levitation went wrong," Lila added. "The only thing I did well was the dream wish."

"There you are then." Cook smiled. "That was something really special."

"But will it be enough?" asked Lila.

Unicorn Dreams

And, of course, no one knew the answer to that.

Cook made a delicious snack of honey cakes and rosehip tart, and Mip told endless jokes, but in spite of everyone's efforts it was to be the longest wait of Lila's life. That night she went to bed early and tossed and turned, unable to sleep for ages.

In the morning she overslept. She was woken by Mip shaking her and Cook telling her to get up at once.

"Your letter's arrived. It's on the kitchen table."

Lila tumbled out of bed and got dressed. When she got to the kitchen, Cook, Mip and the kitchen fairies and elves were gathered around the table waiting for her. A large envelope with an important-looking silver seal sat on the scrubbed boards. It was addressed to *Fairy Lilac Blossom, The Kitchen, Palace of the Fairy King and Queen, Silver Spires* – there was no doubt the letter was for her.

Letters

"Has the Princess received hers?" Lila asked.

"We don't know," said Cook. "But I'm sure we'll hear soon enough. Now go ahead and open yours. We're all bursting to know what it says."

Lila picked up the letter with a trembling hand.

"Now, now," said Cook. "We can't have you looking so miserable. It makes no difference. If you pass the entrance test or you don't, you'll still be the same Lila to me." And she gave Lila a big hug, then sat her down at the table.

Oh, why had she taken the entrance test? Soon everyone was going to know that she had failed.

"I'll open it later," Lila said.

"You'll open it now," said Cook. "The suspense is killing me, and you can't keep the King and Queen waiting. They've asked to hear your results."

Lila took a deep breath and broke the seal on the back of the envelope. A folded paper slid out and opened itself up with an inviting flutter.

"I can't read it," Lila said.

"You must. We're all waiting."

She took hold of the letter with both hands and swallowed hard.

"*Dear Lilac Blossom. I take great pleasure in offering you a place at Silverlake Fairy School,*" she read, without taking in the meaning. She didn't hear the gasps or see the delighted smiles around her. She carried on. "*School starts two moons from the date of this letter...*"

That was as far as she got. An ear-splitting cheer went up from every fairy and elf in the kitchen. Cook's face was alight with the happiest of smiles and she wrapped Lila in a crushing hug, squeezing so tightly Lila could hardly breathe.

"Silverlake Fairy School is only for the best and you are the best! I knew you'd get in."

"What's the rest of the letter say?" Mip asked, bobbing about on the far side of the table.

"Yes, go on," said Cook. "Read the rest."

Lila started again at the beginning because she still couldn't believe the first sentence.

"Dear Lilac Blossom. I take great pleasure in offering you a place at Silverlake Fairy School. Do you think they've got the right Lilac Blossom?" she asked.

"How many Lilac Blossoms do you know that work in the palace kitchen?" said Cook, hardly able to contain her excitement. "Go on."

"School starts two moons from the date of this letter and you will be expected to travel to school in the King and Queen's golden barge. Under no circumstances are new students allowed to fly. A Silverlake Fairy School charm bracelet is enclosed. Please show that you accept this offer by putting the bracelet on your left wrist. But I don't have a bracelet," said Lila, panicking.

Mip reached across the table and shook the envelope. Out dropped a beautiful silver chain. He tried to catch it but it wiggled out of reach

Letters

across the table toward Lila. She picked it up.

"It doesn't have any charms on it," she said.

"You have to earn those," said Cook. "That's what you're going to Silverlake Fairy School for. And I'll tell you something else: it's only you who can wear that bracelet."

"Go on, Lila, put it on," said Mip. "Then you'll know you're going for definite."

Lila slipped the chain over her wrist and the two ends joined together. The bracelet fit perfectly.

"Now, read the rest of the letter," said Cook.

"*The bracelet is your entry pass into the school. Wands will be awarded on arrival. I, and my fellow teachers, look forward to welcoming you to Silverlake Fairy School for the start of the new school year. Best wishes, Fairy Godmother Whimbrel, Headteacher.*"

"Come on," said Cook, almost dragging Lila from the kitchen all the way to the Great Hall.

Unicorn Dreams

She brushed past the Lord Chamberlain and gave a bobbing curtsy to the surprised King and Queen, who were finishing their breakfast.

"She's passed," said Cook, rubbing her hands together, her bright cheeks glowing with satisfaction.

The King nodded. "Well done, Lilac Blossom," he said. "Very well done."

Lila curtsied. The Queen rose and gently raised Lila's chin and kissed her on the cheek. Lila was engulfed by the scent of roses.

"You are a credit to the Royal Palace," the Queen said. "I expect great things of you, Lilac Blossom."

"Thank you, Your Majesty," said Lila, blushing to the roots of her purple hair. She curtsied low and took Cook's hand.

"She expects to do very well, I'm sure," said Princess Bee Balm, with a glittering smile which hid, as Lila already knew, quite different feelings. The Princess had, after all, tried to ruin her chances.

Letters

"I am delighted to tell you that my own dear daughter has also passed the entrance test," said the Queen. "How nice that our two palace fairies will be going to school together. I should like to know how Lilac Blossom does, Cook," the Queen added. "Please, keep me informed."

"I will, Your Highness, and my congratulations to Princess Bee Balm," said Cook. Princess Bee Balm gave Cook a withering look. Cook squeezed Lila's hand and, after one more curtsy, they left the Great Hall.

"That went very well," Cook said, striding briskly along the corridor of statues. Lila fluttered to keep up. "Their Royal Majesties are pleased with you."

"Thank goodness for that," said Lila.

"As for Princess Bee Balm, don't let her bother you," said Cook. "School will sort her out, never you fear."

Lila wasn't so sure, but she was determined not

to let anything spoil the wonderful news of the day. Back in the kitchen she pirouetted around and around the big table. Mip danced behind her, juggling boot brushes. There was laughter and clapping hands and tapping toes as everyone joined in. Cook chuckled over her mixing bowl and pastry cutters, and popped a few flour balls to add to the jollity.

"In two moons I will be going to Silverlake Fairy School," Lila cried happily as she danced. "I will work really hard and one day this beautiful bracelet will be covered with fairy charms." She fluttered her purple wings and spun the bracelet on her wrist. "I can hardly wait!"

Silverlake
Fairy School

For a taste of Lila's next
fairy school adventure, read...

Wands and Charms

Lila had been dreaming of Silverlake Fairy School ever since she had passed the entrance test. It had been a long wait but the first day of school had arrived, and here she was on the riverbank surrounded by her friends and the other First Year fairies, ready to go. She was brimming with excitement. The school was on an island on the far side of the Great Silver Lake, and to reach it they had to travel up the River of Sparkling Waters. *The Golden Queen*, the glittering royal barge belonging to the Fairy King and Queen, was to take them there.

The Fairy Palace had always been Lila's home. Here was everything she knew and loved. She held tight to Cook's hand. Soon they would be saying goodbye for the first time since Lila was a baby. She felt homesick at the thought. If only Cook could come too.

The autumn morning was chilly and the royal party was late. Fairies rubbed their fingers and wiggled their toes to keep warm. Lila hopped from one foot to another, fluttering her purple wings. They couldn't go anywhere until Princess Bee Balm was aboard. It was her first day at Silverlake Fairy School as well.

There was a flurry among the waiting fairies as six prancing white ponies arrived, pulling the royal coach. The driver, an elf in green-and-gold livery, spoke soothingly to steady his team. They had galloped the short journey across the meadow from the Fairy Palace and couldn't understand why they were stopping so soon.

"Better late than never," said Cook huffily.

"It's going to be ages before we see you again, Lila," said Mip, the shoeshine elf and Lila's good friend.

"Mustn't spoil the moment by getting soppy," Cook said, with a catch in her voice. "You going to school is what I've always dreamed of, Lila. But I will miss you something rotten."

"Me too," groaned Mip.

"I'll miss you both terribly and horribly," said Lila, giving Cook a big hug and Mip a kiss on the cheek. The elf turned bright pink but looked pleased all the same.

A footman opened the carriage door and the Fairy King and Queen stepped onto the grass. Those waiting bowed and curtsied. Eager young eyes took in every detail of the beautiful Princess who followed. There were gasps and applause.

Princess Bee Balm was wrapped in a willow-wool cloak of the purest white. From underneath peeked a pink frock, interwoven with threads of fairy gold and silver, that matched the glitter in her pale pink hair. The Princess smiled and, with a graceful nod, acknowledged the greetings.

Lila's new frock matched her wings and hair to perfection and, although she would never have as many clothes as the Princess, today she felt her equal. The dress was a special "going to school" present from Cook and all the other fairies and elves who worked in the kitchen; her tattered old blue one had been dumped in the trash and was gone forever. For once, Lila felt like a princess herself.

"A fair-weather charm," ordered the King. "We can't send the little ones to school in this gloom."

The Lord Chamberlain, stately and dressed in black, stepped forward and raised his silver snake wand. A charm streaked into the sky and spun among the heavy gray clouds until the weak autumn sun broke through. *The Golden Queen* glinted and flamed in the watery light. A large trunk belonging to Princess Bee Balm was carried up the gangplank and placed with the other fairies' luggage on the deck.

"All aboard!" the helmsman cried and the elf-oarsmen took a firm grip on their oars.

Lila's friends from the palace kitchen gathered around her and kissed her goodbye until, last of all, she was swept into one of Cook's bear hugs. It hid the tears that welled up for both of them. Mip solemnly whispered a reminder in her ear.

"Watch out for the Princess!"

Lila nodded. Princess Bee Balm had tried to stop her, a mere kitchen fairy, from passing the Silverlake Fairy School entrance test. She wasn't going to like Lila any better now that they were both going to the same school. Lila would *definitely* watch out for the Princess!

Princess Bee Balm walked regally aboard the shimmering barge and even the golden queen figurehead appeared to turn her head to watch. The new pupils curtsied low. The Princess made her way across the deck and entered the golden cabin. Through the windows, which were open to the air, she could be seen making herself comfortable upon a golden throne. There was a hustle and bustle to be the first on behind the Princess and get a place close to her. Lila waited until the last minute, giving Cook one final hug, before she tripped up the gangplank, her friends waving her aboard.

Lila looked across the river that she loved. She had swum in its sparkling waters often enough and had once, daringly, run her hand along the beaten gold planking of the royal barge as it glided past, wondering what it would be like to sail in such a proud vessel. And now she was.

The helmsman gave his orders and the mooring

ropes were cast off. The great boat drifted away from the riverbank and, to the beat of a drum, the oars dipped into the water and began to pull them upstream.

"Goodbye," Lila called. "Goodbye." There was a tug at her heart and she didn't stop waving until Cook, Mip and her other friends had become a blur of tiny figures. She felt sad to be leaving, but happy to be going too. It was the start of a great adventure.

"What a lot of friends you've got," said a yellow-ocher fairy coming to stand next to her.

"Yes, but I live at the palace," said Lila, dabbing her eyes and smiling. "It was easy for everyone to come and wave goodbye."

"Are you a royal fairy too?"

"No," Lila laughed. "But it feels like it now that I'm wearing a new frock and my Silverlake Fairy School bracelet." She shook the silver chain up her arm. The yellow-ocher fairy was wearing an identical bracelet. It was a sign that they had both been accepted at Silverlake Fairy School.

"My name's Lilac Blossom, Lila for short. What's yours?"

"Nutmeg. Meggie, to my friends."

"Hi, Meggie."

"Hi, Lila." Both fairies smiled and Lila said, "I work in the great kitchen at the Fairy Palace, or I did until today. Cook brought me up. I'm an orphan, you see. It was her dearest wish that I go to Silverlake Fairy School. And mine too. So I took the entrance test. What about you?"

"My parents come from the Spice Islands in the Ocean of Diamond Waters, but now we live on the mainland by the seashore."

"How wonderful," said Lila. "I've always wanted to swim in the sea."

"Swim!" Meggie shivered. "I never swim. My parents want me to learn Spice Islands' charms but that would mean sailing there. I don't even like being on the river. Imagine having to go on a sea voyage!"

"Are the Spice Islands that far away?" asked Lila.

"They're too far for flying," said Meggie. She gently stroked the fabric of Lila's dress. "This is beautiful gossamer. I've never seen such a deep purple before. But then I've never met a purple fairy before either."

"Cook had to have the gossamer specially woven. No one wants to wear such a dark color except me. I think I must be the only purple fairy in the Kingdom."

"And it's such a fine thread!" said Meggie. "When I leave school I want to weave gossamer and make clothes, ballgowns, hats, gloves and shawls." Her eyes shone at the thought.

"Would you make them for me?" asked Lila. "I will always need clothes specially made if I want to wear this color. Would you?"

"It will be an honor."

The two fairies beamed at each other and Lila felt she had made a friend.

To find out what
happens next, read

Silverlake
Fairy School
Wands and Charms

Join Lila and her friends
for more magical adventures at

Silverlake
Fairy School

Wands and Charms

It's Lila's first day at Silverlake Fairy School, and she's
delighted to receive her first fairy charm and her own
wand. But Lila quickly ends up breaking the school
rules when bossy Princess Bee Balm gets her into
trouble. Could Lila's school days be numbered...?

Ready to Fly

Lila and her friends love learning to fly at Silverlake
Fairy School. Their lessons in the Flutter Tower are a
little scary but fantastic fun. Then someone plays a
trick on Lila and she's grounded. Only Princess Bee
Balm would be so mean. But how can Lila prove it?

Stardust Surprise

Stardust is the most magical element in the fairy world. In fact, it's so powerful that all fairies at Silverlake Fairy School are forbidden to use it by themselves. But Princess Bee Balm will stop at nothing to boost her magic...

Bugs and Butterflies

Lila dreams of being picked to play for her clan's Bugs and Butterflies team, and she has a good chance, too, until someone starts cheating! Princess Bee Balm is being friendly to Lila too...so what's going on?

Dancing Magic

It's the end of term at Silverlake Fairy School, and Lila and her friends are practicing to put on a spectacular show. There's also a wonderful surprise in store for Lila – one she didn't dare dream was possible!

www.silverlakefairyschool.com

About the Author

Elizabeth Lindsay trained as a drama teacher before becoming a puppeteer on children's television. Elizabeth has published over thirty books, as well as writing numerous radio and television scripts including episodes of *The Hoobs*. Elizabeth dreams up adventures for Lilac Blossom from her attic in Gloucestershire, England, where she enjoys fairytale views down to the River Severn valley. If Elizabeth could go to Silverlake Fairy School, she would like a silver wand with a star at its tip, as she'd hope to be with Lila in the Star Clan. Like Lila, Elizabeth's favorite color is purple.